This Orchard book belongs to

_____

_____

_____

_____

To Sasha Lois Tilden,
with bubbly chuckles – T.M.

For Natalie,
the mermaid of Cairns – G.P-R.

There are lots of cheeky clown fish hiding in
this book. How many can you spot?

ORCHARD BOOKS
338 Euston Road, London NW1 3BH
Orchard Books Australia
Level 17/207 Kent Street, Sydney, NSW 2000

First published in 2010 by Orchard Books
First published in paperback in 2010

ISBN 978 1 84616 687 7

Text © Tony Mitton 2010
Illustrations © Guy Parker-Rees 2010

A CIP catalogue record for this book is available
from the British Library.

5 7 9 10 8 6 4

Printed in China

Orchard Books is a division of Hachette Children's Books,
an Hachette UK company.

www.hachette.co.uk

Jolly Olly Octopus

Tony Mitton

Guy Parker-Rees

ORCHARD

Underneath the ocean, down beneath the sea,

one wriggly octopus is giggling with glee.

Jolly Olly Octopus laughs away his troubles.
Wriggle-wriggle-giggle – what a lot of bubbles!

Two tickly turtles paddle close by.

They see Jolly Olly. They wave and say, "Hi!"

Jolly Olly Octopus
wriggle-wriggle-wriggles . . .
two tickly turtles both get the giggles!

Giggle-giggle-giggle! Tee-hee-hee!
What a lot of laughter
underneath the sea.

Three smiley sea horses idle on the tide, drifting on the current. See how they glide.

Two tickly turtles, one wriggly Olly,

three smiley sea horses – everybody's jolly!

Four loopy lobsters in a clacky band,
scuttling together across the soggy sand.

They see Jolly Olly dancing in the deep . . .
they all fall together
in a **clicky-clacky** heap!

Giggle-giggle-giggle! Tee-hee-hee!
What a lot of laughter underneath the sea.

Five funny flatfish start to feel flappy.
They flip about, they flop about —
everybody's happy!

Six silly sand eels twist themselves around.
They wriggle and they jiggle
to the bubbly laughter sound.

Seven speedy sea lions come to join the fun.
They turn slippy somersaults one by one.

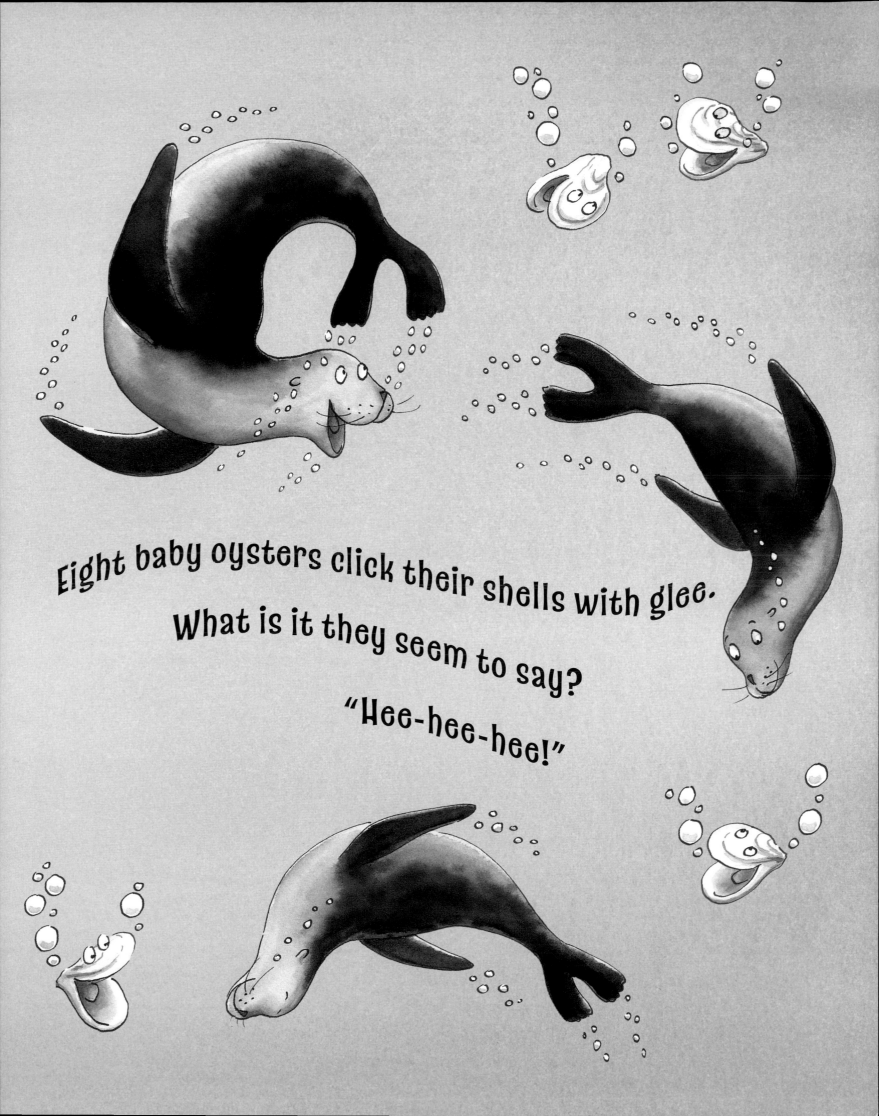

Eight baby oysters click their shells with glee.
What is it they seem to say?
"Hee-hee-hee!"

Nine nifty nautiluses start to jig and grin.

Ten dippy dolphins can't keep their giggles in.

Giggle-giggle-giggle! Tee-hee-hee!
What a lot of laughter underneath the sea.

Suddenly a shark appears!
Everyone goes manic!

The creatures all go crazy in an underwater panic.

The giggles turn to shrieks
and the laughter turns to shock . . .

Where can everybody hide?
Quick! Behind the rock!

Olly's in a tangle and the eels are in a tizzy.
There's flapping and there's floundering.
The water's getting fizzy.
They get in such a fluster as they all start to flee . . .

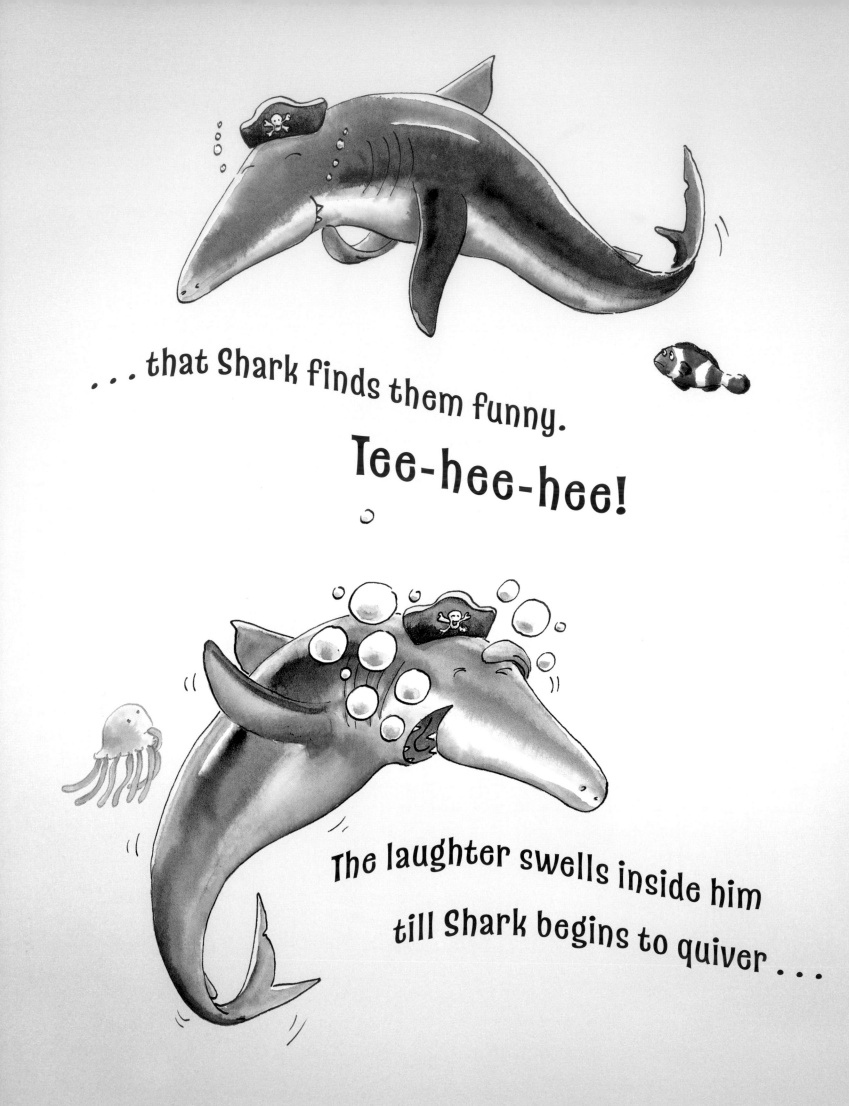

. . . that Shark finds them funny.
Tee-hee-hee!

The laughter swells inside him
till Shark begins to quiver . . .

so bit by bit the creatures see

they have no need to shiver.

Olly starts to caper across the ocean floor . . .